The Adventures of Beatrice and the Bakery Gang

timothy a. bennett

Illustrations by Kalpart

Art Director "timothy a. bennett"

Strategic Book Publishing and Rights Co.

Copyright © 2023 timothy a. bennett. All rights reserved.

Book Design/Layout, Illustrations and Book Cover design by Kalpart.
Visit www.kalpart.com

No part of this book may be reproduced or transmitted in any form or by any means, graphic, electronic, or mechanical, including photocopying, recording, taping, or by any information storage retrieval system, without the permission, in writing, of the publisher. For more information, send an email to support@sbpra.net, Attention: Subsidiary Rights.

Strategic Book Publishing and Rights Co., LLC
USA | Singapore
www.sbpra.net

For information about special discounts for bulk purchases, please contact Strategic Book Publishing and Rights Co., LLC. Special Sales, at bookorder@sbpra.net.

ISBN: 978-1-61204-106-3

Author email id:
info@theadventuresofdogshoeandthebakerygang.com

This book is dedicated to all the "underdogs" of the world.

Dream
Explore
Believe
Stand Up
BE!

DogShoe and I are the same, just like You!

Thank you to the following beautiful spirits;

"Wild Bill" William H. Bennett and Geraldine Moss Bennett, Cindi Bennett Mark and Pauly Beyer, Billy B., Kenneth and Linda Gaddy Moss Family, Howard and Rosalie Bennett Family, Eddie and Marlene Moss Family, Jack and Virginia Bennett Family, Dr. Tamika and Willa Ralston, John Hrycko Family, David and Barbara Lerman Family, Alice Lerman, Sheila "Miss LouAnn" Hawkins, Teri "Linda" and Ben Whitaker, Jenna Hill, Willie and Barb Evans, Bruce, Kalpart and the SPBA Family, Brian Schrader, The Tommy Thompson Family, Scotty and Susi Thompson Family, Joe Rey Family, Guy Anderson Family and DesignTown USA, "The timbennett Supporters" and Todd "Toad Gravel" Grauel".

No Retreat, No Surrender - Bruce Springsteen

peace,

mit

"And rounding the final turn is Sparks, the Burst from Boise; it looks like another bone in his dish tonight," shouted the track announcer, standing on his chair to catch the finish. "Winning by ten links is Sparks! He wins the season championship and receives the Tommy Thompson Championship Trophy Dish filled with assorted racer treats!"

Sparks celebrated his victory by jumping into a massive pile of dog bones and rolling around in them.

"For the fifth time, the Burst from Boise is the champion!"

The Champion, I am the Champion...

Bam! The door slammed, and DogShoe jumped to his paws and realized winning his fifth championship was just a dream.

"It's time to put on your boots and head to the park, boy!"

DogShoe was a sleek, fawn greyhound and former racing star who had paws so sensitive they required protection whenever he went outside. He did not like wearing shoes, and he certainly did not like it when it rained and he had to wear boots.

I cannot wait for the rain to stop, he thought. *I am Sparks, the Burst from Boise. Not DogShoe, the neighborhood laughingstock.*

DogShoe paced on the porch as he waited to go to his favorite place, the Studebaker Dog Park. Drip, drip, drip, the rain pitter-pattered on the roof.

DogShoe had been forced to retire from racing at the peak of his career because of his sensitive paws. After all, a world-class racer could not wear shoes on the track! It was bad enough his racer friends teased him when he wore shoes to practice. Even worse, when the track was muddy, DogShoe had to wear miniature farmers' boots. All the racers and trainers laughed at him. *Why me?*

After retiring, DogShoe was adopted by a very nice family and moved to a small house with a tiny yard. *I Am Sparks*, he thought as he lay down and watched the rain fall from the sky. *Wearing those things on my paws hurts my reputation,* he thought as he rolled onto his back and looked upside-down at his assortment of shoes and boots lined up next to the door.

"Okay, boy, let's hit the road" his owner said.

As they walked the familiar route to the dog park, DogShoe thought about his new home. It wasn't so bad, but he sure missed sprinting around the track and racing his friends to catch that darn bunny. As they passed the Miami Street Bakery, he spotted the neighborhood gang that always cracked jokes about his shoes. *Aw, man, not when I'm wearing the bright yellow farmers' boots*, he thought.

Luckily, they didn't see him, but that was because they were all talking about him. Carson, the yellow-coated alley cat who always had a pair of sunglasses on, was the worst of the bunch.

"I saw DogShoe running back and forth in his little yard. He could barely finish two strides before he hit the fence! Doesn't he know he is too big for that yard?" Carson got up in front of the rest of the gang, took two steps, and pretended to run into the fence and fall down while singing, "Big dog in a tiny yard! Big dog in a tiny yard . . ."

"Well, I think he's cute with that walk of his," said Willa, a beautiful brown-and-white spotted Corgi whose legs were perfectly short for her body. She always came to DogShoe's defense.

"When he walks, he kind of walks sideways and then hops one time. Did anyone see him at the dog park last week? He chased after a squirrel like lightning and got his mouth on it. But then he let it go. He is so fast and cool. You know, he reminds me of someone I have seen before," she said as she nipped at her hind leg.

Carson rolled his eyes and started to lick his tattered coat. *Females could not be reasoned with*, he thought.

DogShoe was thrilled he had gotten past the alley next to the bakery without the usual ribbing. *Mmmm, cookies*, he thought as he sniffed the fragrant air. *One day I will be able to hang out, eat some cookies, and show them how fast I am*. Little did he know, his chance to run was just around the corner.

DogShoe rounded the corner as he had dozens of times before, but this time was different. Old Mrs. Hrycko from down the block was standing in front of her house, waving her hands and yelling, "Burglar! Somebody, help! He's getting away!"

DogShoe broke off his leash and sprinted to her, licking her face and hands to make sure she was okay. *Who would hurt such a nice lady? She always brings treats to the dog park,* he thought to himself, as he heard a loud crash.

DogShoe turned towards the sound and saw a man running from the backyard and turning down the alley. He licked Mrs. Hrycko once more and bolted towards the burglar. He was so fast that he ran right out of his boots and never looked back. "Stop, or I will take you down!" DogShoe barked as he flew down the alley, sending dirt, mud, rocks, and a few cans flying into the air.

By the time the burglar neared the back of the bakery, DogShoe was gaining on him. As they made the turn, DogShoe was going so fast he never saw Carson, Willa, and the others watching in amazement as the blur raced past them.

"That can't be who I think it is," said Carson. The group gathered in the middle of the alley and noticed a collar on the ground.

"Look! This collar fell off DogShoe. 'Property of Sparks, World Record, 2002, 2003, 2004, and 2005'. Who is Sparks, and why is DogShoe wearing his collar?" Carson asked, as he brushed off some mud and tried the collar on for size.

"DogShoe *is* Sparks, you mangy alley cat! I knew he looked familiar! He's the Burst from Boise!" Willa cried as she spun around and jumped excitedly, her short legs unable to get her round body very far off the ground.

"Hey! I am not mangy." said Carson, as he looked at his reflection in the cracked mirror behind the bakery. "Shoot, man, I'm *fiiinnnnne*."

Just then, Sparks caught up to the burglar and cornered him between the bakery and the Green Star Café. The whole gang cheered.

"He caught him!" exclaimed Carson, as they all took off running towards Sparks. "He better not let him go like he did with that squirrel."

Meanwhile, Sparks was barking so furiously he didn't hear them coming. "Don't move or I will bite you, and I have *never* bitten anyone."

Too bad the burglar didn't speak canine. All he knew was that there was a mad dog holding him down, and a gang of his crazy friends were coming down the alley, too. "I don't want any trouble with you or your friends," said the burglar, as he tried to climb the wall to get away.

Sparks had no clue what he was talking about, but he was definitely *not* turning around. He fell for that with Galloping Greg at the track once and ended up with a few fewer racer treats.

"DogShoe, you are my hero," said Willa, as Sparks turned around and realized he had company. The whole gang was there, and all of them were smiling at him! And no one was looking at his boots. *Uh oh*, he thought as he looked down at his bare paws.

"Aww, man, my boots! I am in so much trouble." He took off running back to Mrs. Hrycko's house. "Keep an eye on him, and I will be right back!" he shouted back at the gang, who already had the burglar surrounded.

"Don't you worry; we have him covered," said Carson wickedly, taking out his sharp claws one at a time. The burglar backed further into the corner, terrified.

Sparks arrived back at the house to find Mrs. Hrycko talking with the police, gesturing wildly with his boots in her hands, while pointing down the alley. She spotted him and shouted, "There he is! That's him!" The police pulled their guns, turned around and pointed them at Sparks.

They think I did it! Are you kidding me? I'm out of here! He backed up slowly and then turned around and headed back towards the gang, hoping the police would follow him. Maybe he could lead them back to the bad guy while he made his own getaway.

Sparks sprinted down the alley and went right past the gang with a whoosh of wind and mud.

"Now, where is he going? I thought he was coming back."

Carson was interrupted by the wail of a police siren.

"Great, he brought the cavalry!"

The police car came to a screeching halt. The officers couldn't believe their eyes. Surely their robbery suspect wasn't being held captive by a bunch of household pets!

"Help me, please! I give up! I robbed that lady's house," the man shouted to them. "Just get me outta here! These cats and dogs are animals!"

"Who is he calling an animal?" asked Willa from her perch on an old milk crate. Carson laughed and headed down the alley to look for Sparks.

Carson found DogShoe behind a dumpster in an old abandoned garage, lying between some boxes with a paw over his face. "What's up, Flash?" asked Carson as he sat down and started cleaning himself. He gacked at the taste of his own scruffy fur.

"What do you want?" Sparks looked up, frightened, "Did the police follow you here? Are you turning me in?"

"Naw, don't worry about them; they're busy with the bad guy." Carson put a paw on Sparks's shoulder. "I have never seen anyone run so fast in my life. Well, maybe I saw it on TV," he said, sitting back and admiring his claws. "Nope, on second thought, I have never seen anything like you, *Sparks*." Carson twirled the lost collar in DogShoe's face, got up and walked towards the door leading to the alley.

"Where are you going? And what do you know about me?" In a flash, DogShoe was in front of him, blocking the exit.

"Take it eaaaaasssssssy, I am looking for the gang. I'll bet they can't wait to see you. Listen, the police are not after you. You chased and caught the burglar. You are a hero! People are probably looking to shake your paw, give you an award, and maybe give you some new shoes," Carson said, laughing as he dodged DogShoe and slid out the door. "New shoes for DogShoe . . . new shoes for DogShoe. . . hey, maybe I can pick them out. Ha!" he sang as he started down the alley.

With a big commotion, the door to where DogShoe was hiding flew open, and in came the gang, along with his owner, the police and people carrying TV cameras.

Hey, what is going on? Why are you here? Who invited them? DogShoe was heading for the door when he was stopped by Willa.

"Where do you think you are going? These people are here to thank you for saving the woman and catching the robber. Now, Sit!"she ordered.

He quickly obeyed and sat down with a thump as everyone rushed over to him. They asked his owner and Mrs. Hrycko questions, shook his paw and offered him delicious treats.

The gang beamed as DogShoe looked over, tilted his head a little and winked at his new friends. *Now I'm part of the Bakery Gang which is better than catching that darn bunny!*

Later, in the alley behind the bakery, Carson sat and finished cleaning his sunglasses. "Was life always this exciting for you?" he asked, as he climbed on top of the blue delivery racks. "You are a four-time world-champion racer, you were on TV all the time, and now you save a woman when she gets robbed. I guess that is the life of a star."

Carson and Willa started playing with a box as the rest of the gang resumed their normal positions and DogShoe lay down, happily rolled over onto his back and watched his new friends.

This is better than being a star; now I have real friends who like me, I get bakery treats when we are good and the neighborhood is safe. How could anything be better? DogShoe thought as he looked at the gift Mrs. Hrycko bought for him: a new pair of bright purple running shoes with huge sparkly letters which read, "Sparks." *I knew I should not have let Carson add glitter to my shoes,* He shook his head and rolled his eyes.

See you next time as DogShoe and the Bakery Gang hit the Studebaker Dog Park . . .

We'd like to know if you enjoyed the book.
Please consider leaving a review on the platform from which you purchased the book.

CPSIA information can be obtained
at www.ICGtesting.com
Printed in the USA
BVHW012249100123
656071BV00027B/394